Ace and Christi Series

Summer Fun
with Ace and Christi

by
Grace Whitehart

Illustrated by
John Truman

REACHING THE WORLD FOR CHRIST...ONE CHILD AT A TIME

ACCELERATED CHRISTIAN EDUCATION®
SCHOOL OF TOMORROW®
Hendersonville, Tennessee

This book reflects the frame of reference and ideology
of Accelerated Christian Education, Inc.

Accelerated Christian Education
P.O. Box 299000 • Lewisville, Texas 75029-9000
P.O. Box 2707 • Hendersonville, Tennessee 37077-2707

Reprinted 2019
©1995 Accelerated Christian Education,® Inc.

ISBN 978-1-56265-018-6
11 12 13 14 15 Printing/Year 23 22 21 20 19
Printed in the United States of America

Table of Contents

Making Summer Plans

*My son, hear the instruction of
thy father, and forsake not
the law of thy mother.*
Proverbs 1:8

Ace opened his sleepy eyes and yawned widely. "What day is it?" he thought. Then he remembered. It was the first day of summer vacation! Summer vacation, and just what was he going to do for the whole, long summer? Of course, he was going to visit Grandpa and Grandma Virtueson on the farm for two weeks. But that wasn't until next month. He could hardly wait to see Baba again. Then there would be one week at Bible Camp. Racer and Pudge were going too. Would they have fun then! Yes, fun for a few days, but what about all the other days?

He threw back the sheet and blanket and slowly crawled out of bed.

Standing up, he stretched lazily, took a deep breath, and stepped over to the window. Pushing back the curtain, he could hear the birds singing and see the sun just coming up over the hills, and a soft, warm breeze was gently brushing and tickling the leaves on the big oak tree.

"A whole summer of beautiful days, but what am I going to do for so long?" he said out loud.

Pulling some play clothes out of one of his drawers, Ace dressed, made his bed, and went downstairs to the kitchen. Mother was there to give him a big hug, and as Mr. Virtueson came through the door, he said, "I'm surprised to see you up so early on the first day of vacation, Ace. You must have big plans for today."

"No, I don't," mumbled Ace, ". . . and I'm afraid it's going to be a long summer. Right now I only have plans for three weeks."

Mr. Virtueson looked thoughtful but didn't say anything. Mrs. Virtueson set a big stack of steaming pancakes on the table. As they all took their places around the table, Mr. Virtueson opened the Bible, read a verse of Scripture, and led in prayer.

After prayer, Mr. Virtueson reached for the stack of pancakes and said, "Ace, were you listening to the Scripture I read this morning?"

"Yes, sir. It was Matthew 6:34. 'Take therefore no thought for the morrow: for the morrow shall take thought for the things of itself.'"

"Well, don't you think that could be true for the long summer? I believe that Scripture means we should not be worried about what we're going to do tomorrow . . . or do every day of the summer. True, God wants us to make some plans for the future, but He also wants us to think about just one day at a time."

"I hadn't thought about it that way, Dad." Then Ace became thoughtful for a moment. "God's Word always has an answer, doesn't it? I shouldn't be worried about *all* summer. I have some plans. Right now I'll just think of something to do today."

He stopped just long enough to catch his breath and then asked, "May Racer come over and play with me? He's my best friend, and I miss seeing him already."

"Well, it sure didn't take you long to come up with an idea," chuckled Mr. Virtueson. "That will be fine, if his parents give their permission. However, for part of the day, plan to help Mother in the garden, and maybe Racer can help too. She needs some strong men to dig holes and help do some planting."

"Great!" exclaimed Ace. "This will be fun. I just know Racer will want to help. We'll be done in no time. It won't be hard at all."

"Don't be so sure about that." Mr. Virtueson grinned and gave his wife a knowing look. Ace did not notice. Was there something they weren't telling him?

Would Ace, being so excited, have understood anyway?

After breakfast was over and Dad had left for the church office, Ace called Racer to see if he could come to play. When the phone rang at the Loyaltons, Racer answered.

"Hi, Racer," said Ace cheerily.

"Hi, Ace," answered his friend, not so cheerily.

Ace continued, "Do you think you could come over today? I have a surprise. I'm going to help Mother in the garden. Would you like to help? Ask your parents . . . quick!"

Racer ran to ask and hurried back with the good news. "They said I can," he announced happily. "Dad will drop me off about ten o'clock. I'm really glad you called. I didn't have anything to do. What are we going to do for the whole long summer?" Ace didn't answer his friend's question. He really didn't have an answer, but at least he had plans for today.

After Ace hung up, he hurried to see if Mother was ready. He could see she was, for she had on her big, brown straw hat to shade her face from the sun.

When they got out to the garden, Ace asked, "What can I do, Mother? Dad said I was to help you, and I want to help."

"Well, first of all, I need some holes dug so I can set out these tomato plants. You can do that to help. I'll make a mark with my foot where I want each hole; then you can dig the hole. Make each hole deep—deep enough to set this flowerpot in it—and shovel the dirt into a neat pile at the side. Try to keep the holes in a straight line," she instructed, "so the row will be straight. Use the spade. It's over there against the fence."

Ace went and got the spade. It wasn't a big one, but it was heavy for a little boy. His mother marked the spots for the holes, and Ace began to dig. He dug the first hole nice and deep and piled the dirt from the hole neatly to one side. He moved on to the next hole and did the same. After he had dug about six holes, he stopped. This was hard work! Harder than he had thought . . . and he had six more holes to go. He wiped his forehead and diligently kept going. Finally he finished all twelve holes. By now his back hurt a little bit, and he felt thirsty. "May I go into the kitchen and get a drink?" he asked, calling to his mother at the other end of the garden.

Mrs. Virtueson noticed how hot Ace looked. That knowing look passed across her face again. "Certainly," she answered.

As Ace started toward the back door, he also looked at the holes he had dug. First, he noticed that they did not line up in a nice, straight row. Then, he saw that he had not dug the last holes as nice and deep as the first ones. Also, the dirt from each of the last holes was not piled up neatly as was the dirt beside the first holes. "I didn't do a very good job, . . ." he thought, "but

I'll fix them after I get a drink. Whew, it's hot!"

When Ace was in the kitchen, he noticed that it was almost ten o'clock—time for Racer to arrive! Ace hurried back out to the garden. He wanted to fix the holes before Racer got there and before Mother noticed that he had not followed her instructions very well.

Just as he was finishing up the last hole, Ace heard a car pull up. "Oh, boy! Racer is here," he shouted.

"Well, let's go greet him before you pop a button or something worse," chuckled his mother. "You act as if you haven't seen Racer in weeks, instead of just yesterday at church."

Ace dropped his spade and took off across the yard.

"Wait!" called his mother. Her voice sounded almost like a warning. "Come back here and stand the spade up against the fence. You don't want Racer to step on it and hurt himself. Someone else could trip over it too." Ace ran back, but as he did, he wondered, "Why is it so important to do that now? Couldn't it wait just a few minutes? Just until after I meet Racer?" However, his mother had instructed him to do it, so he obeyed.

It really didn't take any time at all for Ace to get to the front yard. Racer was just getting out of the van.

"I'm so glad you came. I'm already helping Mother plant the tomato plants. It's fun! Now that you're here, we'll be done in no time, and we'll have lots of time to play."

"Yes," answered Racer. "No sweat. Ha! Ha! Race you there!"

The two of them were about to race off, when Mr. Loyalton stopped them. "Not so fast," he said to Racer. "Be a good helper to Ace, and do everything just as Mrs. Virtueson tells you. Don't track dirt in on Mrs. Virtueson's clean floor either. I'll be back to get you before supper."

"Yes, sir," replied Racer, but he was only half listening as he ran off with Ace.

Mrs. Virtueson followed the boys back to the garden. Ace was already showing Racer the nice holes he had dug and was explaining how the row had to be straight and the dirt piled neatly to the side. Racer thought the holes looked super, and he told Ace just that.

Then Mrs. Virtueson called the boys over to the side of the garden. "Ready to help?" she asked.

"Ready!" they answered at the same time and laughed at themselves. They were so funny, and it was good to be doing something together.

"Okay," said Mrs. Virtueson. "Ace, you take this bag of plant food and put one scoopful in each hole. Racer, you follow Ace and pour a little water in each hole—not too much, just enough to make the ground wet. Like this." Then she poured a little water in so Racer could see exactly what she meant. "Don't slop the water on the ground. Just pour it into each hole."

The boys started down the row. Ace scooped out the plant food—one scoopful for each hole. Racer followed. At first he was very careful, but as the boys got to talking and laughing, Racer was not so careful. He was slopping water where it shouldn't be, and water was standing in some of the holes because he had poured in too much.

Soon Mrs. Virtueson asked, "Are the holes ready?"

"Yes, ma'am," answered the boys again, together. They laughed some more. Gardening wasn't nearly so hard when you could do things together.

"Now," said Mrs. Virtueson, "we're ready to set the plants in their holes. Here are the plants. Watch as I put in the first one." Mrs. Virtueson knelt by the nice hole Ace had dug. Gently she bumped the bottom of the little pot. She did not want to hurt the healthy plant that dropped out. She set the little plant in the hole, held it in place with one hand, and pulled the soft, warm earth around it with the other hand. After pressing the ground down around the plant, she stood up and said,

"Now you boys try it. Handle the plants with care. They are just baby plants."

Ace took a little pot, and Racer took a little pot. Carefully they followed Mrs. Virtueson's instructions. When they were finished, three little plants nodded in a straight row.

"You did a good job!" announced Mrs. Virtueson. "Now I need to get a place ready to plant these seeds. Do you think you can follow my instructions and handle this job?"

"Sure," answered Ace. "We'll be done in no time."

Mrs. Virtueson went to the other end of the garden, and the boys got busy.

"This is so easy we'll be done in no time," repeated Racer as he plopped a plant into a muddy hole. As he started pulling the soil around the plant, though, he began to understand why Mrs. Virtueson had instructed him to pour just the right amount of water into the hole and not to slop. The dirt was no longer soft and warm. It was sticky and gooey. "Ace, I think I need to wash my hands," said Racer.

"Well, let's finish first," replied Ace.

The boys continued working, and it wasn't long before both had muddy hands. The mud was harder to work with than the soft soil, and soon they were getting hot and thirsty. "Let's go get a drink," suggested Racer.

"Good idea," answered Ace. The two of them headed for the kitchen. At first they didn't notice that mud was also sticking to their shoes and the knees of their pants where they had been kneeling. Just as Racer opened the door and dashed inside, Ace did notice.

"Stop, Racer!" called Ace . . . but it was too late. Mud was already on the clean kitchen floor.

"Oh, no," fretted Racer. "Dad warned me not to track in dirt . . . and what's your mother going to say?"

"Probably that we have to clean it up," said Ace. "We'd better go tell her."

Of course, Ace was right. So, for the rest of the afternoon—after they had finished planting the tomato plants in the hot sun—Ace and Racer had to clean the mud off their clothes and scrub the kitchen floor. That left very little time to play.

When Mr. Loyalton came to pick up Racer, he asked his son, "Did you have fun today?"

"We had some fun, and we learned some things too."

"And what's that?" asked Mr. Loyalton.

"First of all, planting a garden is hard work . . . , and following instructions gives you more time to play."

Mr. Loyalton looked at his son in puzzlement. He wasn't exactly sure what Racer meant about how following instructions gives you more time to play . . . but we are!

A Backyard Adventure

The eyes of the Lord are in every place, beholding the evil and the good.
Proverbs 15:3

"Hi, girls," said Mrs. Lovejoy as Sandy, Becky, and Christi came skipping into the kitchen. Sandy and Becky were visiting with their friend Christi while their parents were on a business trip to Terra City. "You've been playing out there in the backyard for quite a while. How about some juice and a little snack?"

"Yes, please," they all cried, clapping their hands in glee.

As Mother was getting the snack and juice, she asked, "What have you been doing? You certainly seemed busy out there."

"Well, we played on the swing set for a little while," answered Sandy.

"Yes," agreed Becky, "and Christi pushed me on the swing till I went high. I was

almost flying! It was fun, wasn't it, Christi?"

"It was fun for you, Becky, but it made me tired!" exclaimed Christi.

"I know," continued Becky. "I wanted to swing more, but Sandy wanted to play house. Sandy always wants to play house. She always wants me to be the baby too. Why do they always want me to be the baby?"

"I suppose it's because you are such a sweet little person," replied Mrs. Lovejoy.

Christi and Sandy smiled at each other. They knew Mother understood.

"Do you girls have the little tea set out?" asked Mother. "Would you like to take this peanut butter snack outside and have tea with your dolls?"

"Oh, that would be fun!" agreed the girls happily. "May we take some juice to put in the little cups too?"

"I suppose so," said Mother. "It wouldn't be much of a tea without something in the teacups, now, would it?"

So Mother put all the little peanut butter snacks and a small pitcher of juice on a tray and handed it to Christi. "Here you go," she said. "Have a nice tea."

As Mother watched out the kitchen window, she could see the happy girls having a lovely tea with their dolls. Christi carefully poured the juice into the little cups, and Sandy put a peanut butter snack on each little plate—even on each dolly's plate.

While the girls were having tea, Mother started supper for her family. Now and then she looked out the kitchen window to check on the girls. Soon they brought the empty tray and pitcher back into the kitchen. Everything was gone—even the dolls' snacks.

"Mother," said Christi, "that was really fun. We like pretending we have a home with our dolls. There is only one thing that would make it more fun."

"What's that?" asked Mother.

"We need a house," answered Christi. "We have dishes so we can have pretend tea parties and beds for the dolls to sleep in, but we have no house. How can we make a house—a house with a roof?"

"What kind of roof does your house have to have?" asked Mother. "Does it have to be a flat roof? Can it be a sloped roof?"

"Oh, yes," nodded the girls quickly. They agreed. "A sloped roof would do just fine."

"Okay," said Mother. "Supper is in the oven. Now, you go back outside and move your dolls between the trees. I'll be out in just a jiffy."

The girls scrambled out the door. Now their dolls would have a house. A house with a real roof . . . and not just any roof. Their dolls would have a house with a sloped roof.

Almost before they could get all their dolls and the doll things moved, Mother came out the kitchen door. But what was this? Mother was carrying old blankets and a long rope.

"What are the blankets and rope for?" asked Christi. "We don't need beds. We need a house with a roof—a nice, sloped roof."

"Just wait," said Mother. "You'll see!"

As the girls and Mother worked together, the house began to take shape. Christi tied the rope tightly between the big trees. Then, the girls held the blankets while Mother stretched them over the rope. When the blankets had been fastened in place, the girls squealed with delight. Their house was beginning to really look like a house.

Christi went into the garage and found some cord and little wooden stakes. Mother fastened the stakes to the edges of the blankets so the tent would be secure and the girls would have room inside their house.

As the girls stepped back to admire their house, they could see that it was truly lovely. It had a roof—a tall pointed roof, and the roof had long sloped sides— just as Mother had promised.

"It's wonderful!" exclaimed Sandy. "Thank you, Mrs. Lovejoy, for helping us."

"Let's move the dolls in right away," urged Christi excitedly. "There is so-o-o-o much room. I can't believe we have such a wonderful house. I can even stand up inside our house."

Becky, however, was looking a little puzzled. Mrs. Lovejoy noticed.

"Becky, what's the matter? Don't you like your house?"

"Where's the door?" Becky asked. "How can it be a house without a door?"

"Your house has two doors," said Mrs. Lovejoy, pointing to the openings at each end.

"No." Becky shook her head. "Those aren't doors. You can close doors."

"Oh, I see the problem," said Mrs. Lovejoy. "How about if we do this?" Then she took two more old blankets and hung them at each end of the girls' "house."

"Yes," answered Becky. "That's a door because you can open and close it." And

she pulled the blanket aside and stepped inside the house.

"Are you all set now?" asked Mother, looking at the girls.

"Yes, yes," answered the girls. "Everything is fine now."

"I'd better get back to fixing dinner then," said Mother, turning toward the kitchen.

Inside their house the girls were busily putting everything in place. They put the doll beds on one side and the table and tea set on the other side. And they still had room to move around and play. They were having a great time! Everything seemed perfect now. Nothing would spoil their fun.

About that same time, Susie came down the street on her bike. She thought she might play with Christi. She didn't know Sandy and Becky were already visiting Christi. She dropped her bike in the middle of the walk, pranced up to the door and banged on it. As Mrs. Lovejoy opened the door and saw Susie, she smiled pleasantly and said, "Well, hello, Susie. How are you?"

"Is Christi home? I came to play with her."

"She's in the backyard, Susie, with Becky and Sandy. They're playing house. You may go through the gate and play with them. They have something new I know they'll want to show you."

Susie dashed around to the side of the house, pushed the gate open, and ran through. She was so eager to see what new thing Christi had that she didn't even shut the gate. When Susie saw the nice house that the girls had, she ran over to it and quickly pulled back the blanket door.

"Say, this is really neat! I want to play, Christi. Aren't you glad I came to play?"

"Yes," Christi answered. "I'm always glad when my friends come to play. You may sit here. Would you like to dress this doll? We are pretending that we are going shopping."

Susie took the doll, then snapped, "I don't like this doll. I want that one." She pointed and reached for Sandy's doll.

"You may have this doll," Sandy said agreeably. "Her name is Ann. I have been playing with her all day. Give me your doll. I will dress her."

The girls happily continued dressing their pretend children. "Becky, give me that doll hat," demanded Susie, grabbing for the hat that Becky had in her hand. "I need it."

"But I wanted to put it on my doll," insisted Becky. She started to pull the hat away to keep Susie from having it. Then she remembered something—something she had learned when they were making the house. "Okay, Susie," she said. "There are other doll hats. My dolly, Debbie, will look just fine in this one." She held up a pretty, little blue hat.

Then Susie had an idea. "Let's have a tea party," she said. "I'm hungry. Christi, ask your mother to fix us a snack."

"We have already had a tea party," said Sandy, not waiting for Christi to answer. "Besides, Christi's mother is busy getting supper ready now."

"Sandy, you are mean," shouted Susie. "Everything I want to do, you don't want to do. Why don't you go home? Christi doesn't want to play with you anyhow."

"That's not so, Susie," replied Christi quickly. "I want to play with you and with Sandy. Besides, she can't go home. She is staying the night because her parents are out of town. You are welcome to play too, but we can't ask Mother to fix another snack."

With that, Susie jumped up angrily and threw down Ann. "You don't like me either, Christi! You'll be sorry you didn't want me to play." As Susie ripped back the blanket door, she yanked one blanket off the rope and kicked meanly at the stake that was holding it. When she did, one side of the house caved in on the

33

girls. "There!" she said. "I guess I fixed your old 'house'!"

When Mother saw what was going on, she came rushing out. "What happened? Why did Susie run out of the yard? Why did she kick the stake?"

"Susie got angry because we wouldn't ask you to fix another snack, and she said Sandy should go home."

"I am sorry to hear that," said Mother sadly. "We need to pray for Susie. She needs to understand God's love. You know, I was going to ask her to stay for supper."

"Is Daddy home yet?" asked Christi. "I know he will want to see our fine house. Mother, will you help us fix it?"

"Of course," answered Mother, "but I will need you to give me a hand."

The girls helped, and sure enough, the house was shipshape by the time Mr. Lovejoy came out the kitchen door and greeted the girls. He gave Christi a big hug. "Hello, Sandy and Becky," he said, patting each gently on the head.

"Daddy, how do you like our house?" asked Christi. "Isn't it nice? It has a high roof and sloped sides. It is a nice, cozy place for our dolls, but there is plenty of room for us too."

"I'd say it is a really fine little home," announced Mr. Lovejoy. "It reminds me a lot of a tent my brothers and I once made, only we didn't play dolls in our tent."

"What did you play in your tent?" asked Sandy with interest.

"Oh, we pretended that we were on a camping trip. We pretended we were in the deep northern forest, and we were hunting bears. We even decided to sleep out in our tent."

"Sleep out!" cried Sandy. "What a wonderful idea!"

"I never thought about sleeping out," added Christi, "but it would be fun."

"Well, before you make any big plans," announced Mother, "let's go in and eat supper. It's all on the table. You girls get washed up."

"Yes, ma'am," they echoed each other.

When the family and guests gathered around the table that night, there was much conversation and excitement. The girls told Mr. Lovejoy all about the fun they had having a tea party and how Mother helped them make their perfect house.

Sandy and Christi didn't forget the idea of sleeping out either. "May we?" they asked.

"I hope I won't be scared!" confessed little Becky.

"Well, we may have an answer for that," announced Mr. Lovejoy. "I think I could sleep on the back porch. That way you girls would know I was near."

"You have Somebody else to watch over you too," reminded Mother.

"Yes, we did forget that for a moment, didn't we?" said Sandy. "God and Mr. Lovejoy will both watch over us."

As soon as supper was over, Christi and Sandy helped Mother clear the table and do the dishes. Then they went to get the things they would need for sleeping outside. They had their teddy bears, their Bible storybooks, their sleeping bags, and, of course, a flashlight. Daddy Lovejoy helped them carry everything out to the blanket house and showed them how to fix their beds. The dolls and the tea set were moved indoors so the girls could all fit into the tent.

The sun had already set, and as they were busily preparing for the night, the girls kept the flashlight burning so they could see. They did not notice that it was getting darker outside. They didn't hear Mr. Lovejoy bring his sleeping bag out to the porch and bunk up on the porch furniture either.

When Christi finally looked outside, it was very dark, and most of the lights were out in the house. "Oh-h," she said, "it's dark out here. I'm glad we have the flashlight."

Then Sandy whispered in a rather frightened voice, "I think some animal is out there. Do you hear it?" The girls listened. Yes, they could hear it moving. Just then Patches pushed under the edge of the blanket.

"Oh, Patches," Christi sighed, "you sound much bigger and fiercer in the dark." Patches just snuggled up next to Becky and began to purr.

"What's that?" said a startled Becky and Christi together as they sat up suddenly. The girls listened. There it was again.

"Z-z-z-z."

"Sh-h-h," whispered Sandy.

There it was again! "Z-z-z-z."

"Oh," laughed Christi in relief. "That must be Daddy snoring!"

The girls lay down in their beds. They had never noticed how many strange sounds there were outside at night. Some of the noises were scratching noises, some were scraping noises, some sounded like things flying. They were glad they had the flashlight. It helped. But the light was getting dimmer and dimmer.

Just then there came a big crash, and the wind began to blow hard! "Agh-h!" they screamed.

"Becky, Sandy, Christi," yelled Mr. Lovejoy. "Come in. A storm is coming up!" He ran out into the yard toward the tent. The girls were already running for the back porch with their teddy bears and

Bible storybooks in hand. Another crash of thunder and big drops of rain hurried the girls inside just as Mr. Lovejoy followed with the blankets, sleeping bags, and flashlight.

"Well, so much for sleeping out tonight," said Mr. Lovejoy. "Maybe another time, girls."

"That's okay," announced Christi. "I think we'd rather sleep inside now. I know

the Lord was watching over us," she snuggled close to her father, "but I can feel you."

A Surprise for Pudge

*He that covereth his sins
shall not prosper.*
Proverbs 28:13

"Hi, Pudge," called Grandfather Resource as he rounded the corner of the trailer and walked into the backyard. He had just come back in the jeep from his rounds in the forest. He looked tired, but he was smiling. "How's the fort coming?"

"Come and see," replied Pudge, as he proudly led Grandfather over to four posts standing straight up in the ground.

"I got all the dirt into the holes around the posts, and I packed the ground real hard to make a smooth dirt floor. What do you think?"

Grandfather Resource walked over to take a closer look. "You did a good job, son. I see you put all the tools away too. That's important. I thought we might do some more work on this fort of ours tonight after supper. What do you think about that?"

"Wow! That would be great!" exclaimed Pudge. "I'll go see if supper is ready so we can get started soon."

"No, that's not necessary," replied Grandfather. "I've already checked. We have about ten minutes before your grandmother has supper ready. In the meantime, I have something to show you. Come with me to the jeep."

The two of them walked to the driveway. When they reached the jeep, Grandfather said, "Look in the back."

Pudge jumped up on the back of the jeep and looked more closely. He tried not to let the disappointment show on his face, but sadly he said, "All that's here are some old fence boards. What are they good for?"

"You'll see," answered Grandfather. "Those old fence boards are going to be the sides of our fort. They were trashed when a

new fence was built on the other side of the treeline. They'll be perfect."

"They will?" said Pudge with a question in his voice. "I don't see how they can be the sides of our fort." He was somewhat puzzled.

"Look," said Grandfather pulling one of the boards out of the jeep. "We'll stand them up like this and nail them in place. The pointed top will be perfect for a fort."

"Oh, now I see!" exclaimed Pudge excitedly. "They <u>will</u> be perfect. When can we get started?"

"You remember what I said—after supper."

Just then, Dusty ran out of the woods, and Grandmother came out of the house to tell them that supper was nearly ready. She looked into the back of the jeep. "Why, you're right, dear! These will be just right for the fort! And I can see that Pudge thinks so too!" she said, looking at Pudge's excited face. Then she reached down and patted Dusty on the head.

"Pudge, I think Dusty has a built-in clock. He can be in the woods all day with Grandfather, but he always knows when supper is ready!"

Pudge laughed, "That's okay, Grandmother. Sometimes Grandfather and I are the same way!" With that, they all marched into the house for supper, leaving a hungry-looking Dusty behind. But he knew he would soon get his supper too.

At the table Pudge didn't have much to say. He just gobbled down his food. Once Grandmother said, "Pudge, slow down, and remember your manners."

"Yes, ma'am," said Pudge. "I forgot because Grandfather and I have a lot to do after supper. Right, Grandfather?"

"Right, young man, but I have to change into some old clothes and take care of a few other things first. Building a fort is a big project, and it takes time. We won't finish it tonight. A big part of the fun of having a fort is building it, you know.

To do the job right will take lots of time, so slow down."

Pudge just couldn't seem to slow down, though. He was excited. As soon as supper was over, he began to pace the floor waiting for Grandfather to get his clothes changed. He couldn't understand why Grandfather had to stop to play with Dusty and talk with Grandmother.

Pudge tried to be patient, but it was so hard. "Grandfather, look," he finally said, pointing to the kitchen clock. "It's almost 7 o'clock."

Grandfather Resource understood, but he said, "Remember, Pudge, you're not the only important one around here. I'll be with you shortly, and we'll work for at least an hour. If you would like, you may begin carrying those old boards into the backyard. That will help get the project started while I get my clothes changed."

"I'll get right at it," said Pudge. He was glad to be doing something. "I'll have those boards in the backyard in a jiffy."

Soon Grandfather came out to see how Pudge was doing. He was in his old clothes now and was ready to work. But Pudge's face was red, and big beads of sweat were dripping off his nose and chin. Worse than that, the jeep was not even half unloaded.

Grandfather Resource smiled with understanding. He pulled a big work handkerchief out of his pocket. "Here," he said, handing the handkerchief to Pudge. "Take a break. Sit down and wipe the sweat off your face. Then we'll carry the rest of the boards to the backyard."

Pudge gladly obeyed, and soon they had all the boards in the backyard and had stacked them neatly.

"Are we ready to start nailing the boards on now?" asked Pudge. "I'll go get the hammer and nails."

"Not so fast," warned Grandfather. "We need more than nails and a hammer. Please go get the toolbox from the work shed."

Pudge found the toolbox and carried it into the backyard.

"Pudge, when we're finished, I want you to put the tools back in the toolbox and put the toolbox in the shed where you found it. Can you handle that?"

"Sure," answered Pudge, but he was only half listening. He wanted to get the fort built—and in the shortest time possible. He wondered why building it had to take so much time. But Grandfather had given an instruction, and he expected Pudge to obey.

Since the matter was settled, the two of them set to work, and soon Grandmother could hear, "Zing! Rip! Zing! Rip!" as well as a few excited barks from Dusty.

"They're sawing," she thought.

Then, "Thump! Bang! Thump! Bang! Thump! Bang!"

"Now they're hammering." Grandmother smiled. It was good to see Pudge and Grandfather working together.

Yes, in no time at all, Grandfather and Pudge had boards nailed from post to post in three rows on two sides. "That will work fine," said Grandfather. "I think that's enough for tonight. Tomorrow, while I'm working around the house and making rounds in the forest, you can nail on a couple of these boards. Can you handle that if I check on you every now and then?"

"Yes, sir," answered Pudge. "I'll have it done in a flash."

"Well, let's do one or two boards tonight so I can show you how to make them straight. Bring me a board from the pile."

Pudge got a board from the pile. He was getting excited. The fort was soon going to start looking like a fort.

"Set the board up on end like this," instructed Grandfather. "Now, you hold it while I drive one nail to hold the board in place. Do you see how I'm doing it?"

"Yes, sir," answered Pudge.

"Next, use this level to check to make sure the board is straight." The tool was rather interesting. It had a little window on the side, and inside the window was a bubble that moved. "Then nail the board at the top, in the middle, and at the bottom." Grandfather showed Pudge how to do it. "Thump! Bang! Thump! Bang! Thump! Bang!"

"Tomorrow, do your boards the same way. Be sure to check each one with the level to see that it is straight; then nail it tight. Work carefully, and do the job right. Do you understand?"

"Uh . . . oh . . . sure, Grandfather," answered Pudge.

"Pudge!" said Grandfather Resource in a commanding tone of voice. "Are you listening?"

"Uh . . . yes, Grandfather." But Pudge was only half listening again. He was picturing in his mind how the finished fort would look.

"It's time to go in now," announced Grandfather. "I'm going to go wash up. Take care of your responsibility with the tools, and come right in."

"Yes, sir," replied Pudge dreamily.

He was thinking of all the fun he would have playing in the fort. For several minutes he just stood there imagining the games he would play. Why, he might even get to invite Ace and Racer to come play in the fort with him sometime. Tomorrow, with Grandfather's help, two sides would be done. It wouldn't take long at all.

Just then Grandmother called, "Pudge, are you coming in?"

"Yes, ma'am," he answered. "I'm coming." He had a pleasant smile on his face. He had an idea for how to make the job go faster.

That night Pudge slept very soundly. He didn't even hear the "pitter-patter" of the mountain rain against his window. He was dreaming about playing with his friends in the fort. What wonderful dreams!

The next morning Pudge wasted no time dressing and finished his breakfast in nothing flat. He remembered how Grandfather had said to drive one nail, then check for straightness, and then pound in other nails to fasten each board tight. Pudge had some ideas of his own, though. He wouldn't have to check every single board to see that it was straight. Also, why couldn't he drive all the nails at the same time? That would save work and time. He could have the job done in no time.

Pudge raced out into the yard to start work. Then he stopped short. There on the ground was the toolbox. He had forgotten to put it away as Grandfather had instructed him to do. The lid was not even closed. The rain had gotten the tools wet, and Dusty had dragged some of the tools out into the yard.

"Oh, dear," thought Pudge. "I'll pick up the tools and put them away tonight for sure. They'll be all right."

Pudge went around and picked up all the tools off the muddy ground and put them in the toolbox. When he finished, he pulled a board over to the fence and set it up in place. Then, without checking to see how straight it was, he pounded a nail in the middle. "Thump! Bang! Thump! Bang! Thump! Bang!" He nailed it good and tight. Then he reached to try to pound a nail in the top, but it was hard to reach. Instead, he pounded two nails in the bottom. "Thump! Bang! Thump! Bang! Thump! Bang!"

"There, it's good and tight," he thought. He was pleased with his work.

For the next hour, Pudge worked diligently standing up the boards and pounding them in place. Grandfather had told him to do only a couple, but he worked hard and was almost through with one whole side. He hadn't checked to see how straight they were, but he had nailed them good and tight. Just then, Grandmother called that she had a little snack ready for Pudge.

He pounded one last nail into one last board. "There," he said to himself. "Won't Grandfather be surprised! I did all he told me to do and more!"

Pudge was glad to get a little rest. When he sat down at the table, Grandmother asked, "Are you tired, dear? It looked as if you were working very hard out there."

"I'm a little tired," replied Pudge, "but I did more than Grandfather thought I could do."

Just then, Grandfather Resource walked in. "Hello, everyone. I got through with my rounds early; so, Pudge, I'm ready to help you work on that fort. How's it coming?"

"Good," Pudge said mysteriously, "and I have a surprise for you." He thought Grandfather would be surprised that he had finished the job so quickly. Pudge hadn't followed the instructions exactly, but he had gotten more done than Grandfather had said to do. He thought that was what really mattered.

However, instead of Grandfather's being surprised, it was Pudge who was surprised.

When Grandfather looked at the fort, he said, "You nailed them good and tight, didn't you?"

"Oh, yes, sir," answered Pudge proudly.

"But did you check to see that each board was straight before you nailed it in place?"

"Well, no," confessed Pudge, "but how did you know?"

"Pudge, look for yourself," replied Grandfather. "Some of the boards slant."

"But I got all the boards on, and they are good and tight; I even put some extra nails in the bottom because I couldn't reach the top," noted Pudge in a voice that seemed to ask for Grandfather to okay what he had done. "Check and see."

"I see," said Grandfather. "I know you worked hard . . . but, Pudge, you did not follow my instructions. It's important to work hard, but it's more important to follow instructions."

Pudge hung his head. He knew he had disappointed Grandfather. How could he show Grandfather that he really was sorry and wanted to do right?

"Pudge," continued Grandfather Resource, "I am glad you wanted to please me . . . and I want to get the fort done quickly too. But the best way to please me AND get the fort done quickly is to follow my instructions."

"Yes, sir. I see that now, Grandfather. I was wrong; I'm sorry."

"I forgive you, Pudge," replied Grandfather. "You need to ask the Lord to forgive you too for being disobedient. I trust you've learned a lesson from all this."

"You're right, Grandfather, and I have learned a lesson," added Pudge. "I'll nail all the rest of the boards just the way you instructed me."

"You will need to do more than that, Pudge, if you want to please me and the Lord," noted Grandfather. Then he pointed to the boards that Pudge had nailed good and tight. "These boards must be pulled off and put on right. We can work on that the rest of the day. I thought we could build another side, but first we must fix what was done carelessly. The other sides will have to wait."

With that, Grandfather Resource reached into the toolbox to get the nail puller. "What's this?" he said with more disappointment in his voice. "The tools are wet and muddy, and there are teeth marks on some of them. Puu . . . dge," said Grandfather looking sadly at his grandson, "did you put away the tools last night?"

Pudge unhappily hung his head again. He wanted to crawl away somewhere and cry. In a very ashamed voice, he said, "No, Grandfather . . . but I <u>will</u> tonight. I promise."

"We need to do more than that," said Grandfather, "and the plans must change again. This afternoon we'll dry out the toolbox and clean all the tools so they

won't rust. Then, after supper we can pull all the boards off. We'll have to start all over tomorrow."

"Oh-h-h," moaned Pudge. "Why didn't I do the job right in the first place? I didn't follow instructions, and I thought you would never know. When we sin and try to cover it up, our plans really get messed up, don't they, Grandfather?"

"The Bible says, 'He that covereth his sins shall not prosper,'" answered Grandfather Resource. "God's Word doesn't lie."

"You can say that again!" added Pudge.

"Okay," agreed Grandfather with a little smile on his face. "The Bible says, 'He that covereth his sins shall not prosper.' God's Word doesn't lie."

Pudge hardly knew whether to laugh or cry. "Let's get to work and start cleaning the tools," he said. "This time I'll do the job right!"

The Big Cover-Up

But whoso confesseth and forsaketh them [sins] shall have mercy.
Proverbs 28:13

As the Virtuesons' car pulled up to the curb in front of Pudge's house, Ace could hardly sit still! Today was the day his family was going to go to Grandpa and Grandma Virtueson's farm. Best of all, Pudge Meekway was going to go also.

Pudge was waiting and seemed just as excited as Ace. He kissed his mother good-bye and helped Mr. Virtueson put the suitcase into the trunk. Then he piled into the back seat with Ace. After they had prayed for God's blessing and safety, they were off.

"Thank you for picking me up," said Pudge politely.

"You are very welcome, Pudge," replied Mrs. Virtueson. "We are glad you could come along with us."

"You can say that again!" cried Ace, wearing his most excited face. "I thought today would never come. At last we are on our way to fun on the farm!"

Ace and Pudge settled back in the seat, buckling their safety belts. Grinning at each other, they began chattering, thinking of all the fun waiting for them on Grandpa and Grandma's farm.

There would be so many things to do. Feed the chickens. Gather the eggs. Fish in the pond. Maybe even go wading in the pond! Sleep in the loft of the barn. Jump into a sweet-smelling haystack. Ride the gentle, old horse. Milk the spotted cow. Climb the big trees. Eat Grandma's hot, fluffy biscuits. Wake up at the sound of a rooster crowing. Yes, without a doubt, they would have fun on the farm! A whole week of fun on the farm!

The time whizzed by as fast as the telephone poles on the side of the road. Soon, Ace began to see well-known landmarks that told him they were getting close to the farm.

"My stomach tells me it's getting close to lunch time!" said Pudge.

Mr. Virtueson laughed as he agreed. "My stomach is growling the same thing."

"Don't worry about eating this week," added Mrs. Virtueson. "One thing is for sure. Grandma loves to cook for her family, and she knows we are coming. There will be plenty of food!"

Turning off the highway onto a long dirt road, they could see Grandpa and Grandma Virtueson sitting in a swing on the big porch that circled the old farmhouse.

"Look," shouted Ace. "There they are! I feel a big hug coming. In fact, I feel two big hugs coming."

As Daddy stopped the car, Ace scrambled out and up onto the porch with his arms flung open. Pudge was right on Ace's heels, hoping for hugs himself.

"Oh, Grandpa. Oh, Grandma. It is so good to see you!" cried Ace as he hugged his grandparents.

"Hello, Ace. Hello, Pudge. Welcome to the farm," they greeted, smiling at the two young boys.

Grandma Virtueson stepped closer to Pudge and said, "Pudge, I have an extra hug and it's just for you."

Pudge smiled shyly as he stepped into Grandma's welcoming arms.

"Uhm-m-m," thought Pudge, "how wonderful that Ace has such a kind grandmother. And it is extra nice that she smells just like fresh-baked biscuits."

Pudge enjoyed the loving welcome of Ace's grandparents. He knew, though, that he would be glad to be here at the farm even if Grandma Virtueson didn't love to cook!

Later, carrying their bags upstairs, Ace and Pudge noticed the old steps creaking. "Sounds like the stairs are also happy we are here!" said Ace.

". . . or maybe the stairs are glad we haven't sat down to eat yet," laughed Pudge.

The boys raced around their room, unpacking their suitcases.

"Ace, do you really think your parents and grandparents will let us sleep out in the barn? I've never slept in a hayloft before, and it would be such fun."

"Daddy said we could. Only . . ."

"Only what, Ace?"

"Only it's dark out there at night. Will you be afraid?" asked Ace.

"Naw," bragged Pudge. "We can take a flashlight, can't we? Besides, the moon will probably be shining."

"Right!" agreed Ace as he sprang toward the door. "The last one down to lunch gets a COLD biscuit!"

That evening, Ace and Pudge went to the barn with Grandpa Virtueson. Old Bessie, the spotted cow, needed to be milked again.

Grandpa tried to teach Pudge how to milk the cow. It was much harder than it looked! Pudge's hands and arms ached, but he felt pleased when he was able to get a little milk into the pail. It was so much fun to learn something new—especially when Grandpa Virtueson was teaching him and praising him for doing a good job.

While Grandpa was finishing the chores, Pudge noticed a box in the corner. "What's that?" he asked.

"Oh, that's a hatcher for the hen's eggs," explained Grandpa.

Grandpa could see that Pudge was interested and did not really know what a hatcher was. He walked over to the hatcher and lifted the cover.

"Look inside, Ace and Pudge."

The boys bent over to look into the hatcher. They stared in amazement. Inside were several eggs being warmed. From the eggs came tiny cheeping sounds!

"Let me show you something," said Grandpa. Then he picked up a strange-looking flashlight and one of the eggs. "This special light helps me to see the chick before it is ever hatched."

Pudge and Ace watched as Grandpa put the light on one end of the egg. The light showed a small form inside the egg, and it was moving! The boys could see that inside each egg was a living chick . . . a chick that had been given life by God. Soon the chicks would hatch from the eggs.

"Perhaps even by tomorrow morning the eggs will hatch," said Grandpa, "and we will have some new baby chicks! You may pet them, but don't pick them up. They can be injured easily."

Both Ace and Pudge thought that would really be something to see and tell about to all their friends back in Highland City!

Later that evening, after each boy had taken a warm, soapy bath in the old, old bathtub that had what Grandma called "claw feet," they headed for the barn, carrying two of Grandma's heavy quilts. Ace also carried a small flashlight tucked into his pocket. Pudge carried a canteen filled with water and a couple of cold biscuits wrapped in a napkin.

What an adventure! What fun on the farm! Climbing the ladder to the hayloft, the boys piled fresh hay as high as their knees. Then they spread the quilts on top of the hay. They felt just like two cowboys from long ago. They were really sleeping in a barn, hearing the horse and cow and chickens below.

Lying on their backs, looking out the window, Ace and Pudge watched the moon and millions of twinkling stars. Being on the farm was so much fun!

Just as Ace was dropping off to sleep, Pudge reached for the canteen and a cold biscuit. Oh! He accidentally knocked over the flashlight, which rolled off the edge of the hayloft!

Clatter! Clatter! Bang! CRASH!

"What was that?" cried Ace as he sat straight up.

"Oh, Ace. That was our only light. I accidentally knocked the flashlight out of the hayloft. It's down there on the barn floor—probably in a hundred pieces, and the moon sure doesn't seem to be bright at all. In fact, it's really dark!"

"It will be all right, Pudge. We are safe here."

"But, Ace, what if there are wild animals around?"

"Pudge, there aren't any dangerous animals around here. Remember, God watches over us all the time, and He has promised to take care of us. Also, don't forget that Grandpa's window is open, and he would be here as fast as you could snap your fingers—if we really needed help."

With that said, Ace lay back down. Seeing Ace's bravery, Pudge, too, lay down—after practicing snapping his fingers once or twice! Both boys were soon fast asleep—even in the dark.

The soft sounds of peaceful sleep soon mixed with the country sounds of chirping crickets and a hooting owl. Somewhere in the old farmhouse, a clock ticked away

the hours as Ace and Pudge slept on their beds of hay.

As he rolled over, Pudge could see the sky was beginning to get light. Was it morning already?

"Cock-a-doodle-doo!" The rooster quickly answered Pudge's question.

It was a new day on the farm! God had taken care of them during the night— just as Ace had said God would. Now that it was morning, Pudge felt a little silly when he remembered being afraid of the dark the night before . . . but, after all, he WAS still learning about God, wasn't he?

Even though Ace was still asleep, Pudge quietly hopped out of bed. He hurried softly down the ladder, for he had something to see!

Running to the corner of the barn floor below, Pudge gently opened the hatcher. Cheeping loudly was one baby chick! One chick with soft, yellow down. One chick right out of his shell into God's world!

Forgetting what Grandpa Virtueson had said, Pudge picked up the little, yellow ball. It was warm and so-o-o-o soft. Then it startled him by pecking at his fingers, and Pudge accidentally dropped the baby chick.

Oh, no! The chick lay still on the ground. The chick lay TOO still on the ground. All at once, he remembered that Grandpa had told him not to pick up the chicks.

"Oh, oh," moaned Pudge as if his heart would break with sadness. "The little chick is dead. I didn't mean to hurt it, but I killed it. What shall I do? I just know Grandpa Virtueson will be angry with me."

As Ace started down the ladder from the hayloft, Pudge clumsily covered the dead chick with hay. He didn't know why, but he tried to hide the chick.

Quickly straightening up, Pudge attempted to look as if nothing were wrong. He said, "Oh, hi, Ace. I was just picking up the broken flashlight."

"I'll help you," said Ace. "Then we can begin another day of fun."

"Yes," mumbled Pudge, but somehow, he already knew this day was not going to be much fun.

After breakfast, the boys played, fished, and waded in the pond. Ace noticed that Pudge didn't seem to be having as much fun as he was.

Climbing up in the biggest apple tree, on a branch alongside Pudge, Ace plucked an apple for each of them.

"Pudge?" he asked. "What's wrong?"

Pudge turned to look at Ace. His eyes were filled with tears, but he couldn't say anything.

"Are you missing your daddy?" whispered Ace, thinking maybe that was the problem.

"I always miss my daddy, ever since he went to Heaven," replied Pudge, "but that's not what's wrong."

"What IS wrong? Tell me," encouraged Ace. "I'm your friend."

So, there in the branches of the old apple tree, Pudge told Ace the sad thing that had happened early that morning. He told Ace how he had accidentally killed a precious baby chick and how terrible he felt about it.

Now Ace knew why Pudge wasn't having fun on the farm today.

"Pudge, you need to tell Grandpa what happened. He will understand, and he will forgive you. I know he will."

"Ace, I can't tell your grandpa. I want him to like me; I really do. He may think I did it to be mean."

"No, he won't, Pudge. I know Grandpa will understand. Come on, I will go with you to tell him," promised Ace.

"But, I can't!" cried Pudge, scrambling down from the tree and running to the barn.

"Wait! Wait for me!" called Ace as he dashed after his friend. Ace reached the barn just in time to see Pudge take the empty eggshell from the hatcher and hide it under the hay too, right where the dead chick was still hidden.

Climbing back into the hayloft, Pudge lay down on his bed of hay and covered his head with Grandma's quilt. Pudge was so sad and miserable. He could hardly remember how much fun he had had yesterday. Today was supposed to be another day of fun on the farm. It wasn't!

At supper that night, everyone noticed that Pudge was hardly eating. He just picked at his food, even letting his fluffy biscuit get cold. When Grandma brought out a homemade apple pie, Pudge wasn't even interested.

Only Ace knew what was wrong. He wanted to help his friend, but Pudge himself had to do what was right. Somehow, Ace had to get Pudge to understand that. As the boys helped Grandma clear the table, Ace silently asked God to help Pudge.

After such a day, sleeping in the barn didn't seem like much fun; so the boys climbed the old, creaking stairs to their room and lay on their bunk beds.

Neither boy could think of anything that sounded fun. Not games, not puzzles, not even the wonderful old books on the shelves.

All Pudge wanted to do was go home, but he knew that was impossible. He and Ace were to stay on the farm all week, and he surely couldn't walk back to Highland City.

Ace knew Pudge was very unhappy, but what could he do for his friend? Silently he again asked God to help.

"Ace," begged Pudge, "please don't tell your grandpa."

"I won't," answered Ace, "because you will have to tell Grandpa yourself. I know you will because it is right. Don't you want to do the right thing?"

"Oh, I do. I do. If only I could . . . ." As Pudge lay there thinking of what he had done, the ticking of the old clock on the wall seemed like little hammers banging in his head.

Then, a soft tapping on the door interrupted Pudge's thoughts.

"Come in," called Ace.

Stepping brightly into the room, Grandpa looked at the boys with smiling eyes, then turned to Pudge.

"Pudge, we are so glad you are here on the farm with us, but it seems you're not having a good time. Are you homesick? Would you like to go home?" asked Grandpa Virtueson.

Pudge looked at Grandpa. He looked at Ace. Then he looked at Grandpa again.

He knew what he must do. He must tell Grandpa the truth—the truth about what had happened in the barn early that morning. In a very small and trembling voice, he told Grandpa the whole, sad story.

Patiently, Grandpa listened as the words tumbled out. Pudge told about how, in his excitement, he forgot that Grandpa had told them not to pick up the chicks, how he tried to cover up the accident, and how miserable it had made him all day. When Pudge finished, in tears, he asked Grandpa to forgive him.

"Pudge, confessing your sin was the right thing to do—and very courageous. I forgive you, and I understand how you feel. I saw the empty shell in the hatcher this morning, and I wondered what happened. I was just waiting for one of you boys to tell me about it. I know you did not mean to kill the baby chick. It was an accident, and I would have forgiven you right away . . . if you had told me right away. Trying to hide the problem is what has been making you unhappy all day.

"In my favorite book of the Bible, Proverbs, there is a verse that I want you to remember. 'He that covereth his sins shall not prosper: but whoso confesseth and forsaketh them [sins] shall have mercy.'"

Looking up into Grandpa's gentle face, Pudge grinned a crooked—but happy—little grin and said, "Thank you, Grandpa Virtueson. Thank you so much for understanding. I will learn that proverb before I go to sleep tonight. Thank you for loving me and teaching me more about God's Word."

Pudge took out his Bible and turned to Proverbs 28:13. Looking over at his friend Ace, he said, "Tomorrow will be a great day! I just know it."

When the boys turned out the light, Pudge lay there listening to the old clock. It seemed to be playing a soft, happy lullaby. Soon Pudge was fast asleep.

Trouble Goes to Camp

Let not thine heart envy sinners.
Proverbs 23:17

Christi and her parents had just arrived to pick up Susie Selfwill. The girls and several other friends were going to church camp!

As Mr. Lovejoy and Christi walked up to Susie's door, a man's voice seemed to boom from behind it, "Take this money and get out of here!"

The two looked at each other in surprise. Then Susie bounced out the door. She was stuffing some money into her new pocketbook and smiling as if nothing had happened. "Hi! I'm ready," she said. Christi was puzzled, but she picked up the happy tone and replied, "Okay! Away we go!"

While they loaded Susie's suitcase into the trunk of the car, Christi noticed tears in Susie's eyes. Had Susie's stepfather said other hurtful things to her?

Christi's heart ached for her friend. Silently, she prayed for the day when Susie's family could be as happy as her family.

Soon Mr. and Mrs. Lovejoy, Christi, and Susie arrived at the church parking lot, and all the sadness seemed to be put aside.

Christi had never seen so many of her friends gathered to go on a trip. In fact, this was the first time most of the "gang" had gone to church camp!

The fathers loaded all the suitcases and bags onto the bus as Christi and her friends talked and ran about excitedly.

Ace, Racer, Pudge, J. Michael, Sandy, Bill, Booker, Reginald, and Happy were all there, as well as Miriam and her cousin, Mitchie. Mitchie had come for a summer visit and was going to church camp too.

Christi just knew she was going to like Mitchie. Mitchie's big, brown, beautiful eyes and shy smile, as bright as sunshine, seemed to say, "Let's be friends."

Christi was glad her friends would be with her at church camp, but she was also pleased to see that Miss Content, Mr. Friendson, and Mr. and Mrs. Virtueson were going too.

What a trip this was going to be! Everyone was laughing and talking as they climbed into the bus and found their seats.

"Grab your pillow," Bill called to Booker.

"We have the cooler," shouted Racer and Ace.

"Let's not forget the snacks," reminded Pudge.

At last, all were ready for the happiest ride of the summer.

After Mr. Virtueson led in prayer, he slipped behind the wheel of the bus.

Christi was as excited as everyone else— until the old bus groaned and started to roll slowly away from the church parking lot. Then, as she waved good-bye to her father and mother, she suddenly had a

lump in her throat that felt as big as a baseball. She wanted to laugh and cry at the same time. She had never before gone away from home for so LONG.

As the bus turned onto the highway, Racer started singing, and the rest of Christi's friends joined in and sang along. "My Lord knows the way through the wilderness, all I have to do is follow . . . ."

Christi was very pleased to notice that even Susie had picked up on the words of the song and was singing almost as loudly as Pudge and Bill. Christi hoped this week at church camp would be a happy one—especially for Susie.

The bus bumped over hills and through valleys, following curves around little towns. The sun shone through the window, and soon the songs faded away. Heads began to bob sleepily. The trip was still fun, but quieter fun.

Christi looked at Susie sitting next to her on the same seat. She was beginning to nod off to sleep. Christi prayed that

Susie, especially, would enjoy the week at church camp. She knew Susie was not as happy as she pretended. It was true that Susie acted mean at times, but perhaps Susie just needed to know that God loved her. One way to help Susie understand God's love was to be a friend to Susie.

As the miles rolled on and the minutes ticked into hours, the tires of the bus hummed their own happy tune. The big, yellow bus swayed back and forth, gently rocking the sleeping travelers.

Pudge was the first to wake up. He quietly asked Mr. Virtueson, "Can we please stop soon? I'm thirsty."

A cheer of agreement came from Reginald and Bill, and that woke up everyone!

Soon Mr. Virtueson pulled the bus into a large truck stop with a gas station, cafe, and gift shop. Being gentlemen, the boys let the girls get off first. Even thirsty Pudge was willing to wait for the young ladies to go first.

Booker and Happy remained outside the bus and watched Mr. Virtueson pump gasoline. Most of the others were interested in stretching their legs and getting some exercise by walking around the gift shop.

It was fun to see all the neat and interesting things, but they just LOOKED. They were all saving their hard-earned spending money for the week at camp. All, that is, except Susie. Pushing into line to pay for her drink, some candy, a bag of chips, a book, AND a travel game, Susie boasted, "I have so much money I'll never be able to spend it!" With that, she went out to the bus, leaving the other girls behind.

Sandy was shocked by Susie's words and thought to herself, "It took me weeks to earn my spending money for this trip. Why should she brag about how much she has?"

Miriam knew Susie's words hurt Mitchie because Mitchie had no spending money. Why did Susie have to be so rude?

Miriam decided she would share what money she had with her cousin. Maybe some of the other girls would do the same. Why didn't Susie think about other people's feelings?

As the group filed back onto the bus, it seemed everyone had forgotten what Susie had said, but everyone hadn't forgotten.

Mitchie watched Susie reading her book, and she felt angry. Why did Susie have so much money to spend? Susie could buy anything she wanted. Mitchie couldn't buy anything. It wasn't fair, and Mitchie felt very envious.

Christi noticed the frown on Mitchie's face and flashed a smile at her. Mitchie remembered that she should be nice to Susie; so, she smiled and settled back in her seat.

Before they knew it, the bus was stopping again—this time along the highway in a shaded picnic area.

In no time at all, some juicy hot dogs were sizzling over a fire. The good smell mixed with the sparks and smoke rising up from the burning wood. "Yum-yum," thought the hungry travelers.

"I'm not sure which smells better, the roasting hot dogs or the burning wood," said Happy, "but I do know which will taste better."

"Right!" agreed Mr. Friendson. "Let's all pitch in and set the table!"

Mr. Virtueson opened the giant jar of pickles. Mrs. Virtueson and Miss Content dished out the cold potato salad from the cooler, and Christi and Sandy poured tall glasses of ice-cold lemonade.

Then they all thanked God for these things He had given them to enjoy.

Fixing a second hot dog for himself, Reginald asked, "Pudge, do you want another hot dog?"

"I'm not sure," answered Pudge. "Why do you ask?"

"Oh, I just thought you might want another one—since you have enough mustard on your face for at least one more."

"Thanks. I think I will," said Pudge with a smile as he reached for another napkin. Wiping his face, he added, "It's okay to laugh. After all, you're the one wearing ketchup on your top lip."

Giggles and laughter again sounded around the picnic tables. It was such fun to be here together with friends! Susie was very clearly having a good time. Even Mitchie laughed out loud. She was feeling part of the group too.

While the fire burned out, everyone helped clean up and load the bus.

Meanwhile, an unseen, small visitor—more nosy than wise—sneaked into the bus from one of the overhanging shade trees. This visitor with four tiny feet was just playing mostly, but he WAS sniffing around hunting for something to eat. Finding a bag of peanuts in J. Michael's backpack, he had lunch too. Like the others at the picnic, his tummy was soon full. Then, deep inside the backpack, he curled up and went to sleep with his bushy tail covering his face.

Returning to the bus—girls first, of course—the group looked forward to the end of their trip.

"Bless the rest of our trip," prayed Mr. Virtueson as they started out. "Bless the coming week that we might learn to love You more. And bless the boys and girls as they learn of the big surprise. Amen."

"Surprise? What surprise?" everyone wanted to know.

"If I told you now, it wouldn't be a surprise tomorrow," teased Mr. Virtueson.

As the wheels of the bus began to turn, everyone sat back and tried to guess what the surprise would be.

It was fun to be together on a bus going to camp. Just talking was fun. Just being together was fun! As everyone chattered about the coming fun of the week ahead, J. Michael happened to look down and notice that his backpack needed zipping; so, he zipped it—not knowing what you and I know!

Christi, Miriam, Mitchie, and Sandy were laughing and talking excitedly when Susie, who had been sitting at the back with Miss Content, noticed that they were having a good time . . . without her.

She jumped to her feet, marched up the middle of the bus, and angrily stared at Mitchie. Keeping her voice low so none of the adults could hear her, she whispered meanly, "Get out of that seat. It's mine!"

Wanting both Susie and Mitchie to feel a part of the fun, Sandy said, "Here, Susie, sit with me. There is plenty of room for all of us. There is always room for one more friend."

"Thanks!" grumbled Susie as she flopped down next to Sandy.

The girls relaxed, and Susie's stormy feelings seemed to pass over. Each girl was determined to be as kind to Susie as she could be—even if it wasn't always easy.

Mitchie, being new to the group and shy, watched but didn't say anything. Her grandmother had often told her that she could learn more by watching and listening than by talking. So she kept her thoughts to herself and moved back to sit with her cousin Miriam.

The young friends kept chattering about all the fun they would have during their week at church camp. "I'm looking forward to the meetings under the big tent—especially the puppet stories," said Miriam excitedly.

"I can't wait to see what crafts we make. I want to make something really special for Daddy and Mama," added Christi.

"Do you think we'll have a cookout?" asked Sandy.

"I'm going to be the first in the swimming pool and the first to hike up the mountain," said Susie.

"I'm excited about . . ." began Mitchie.

"About what, Mitchie? What are you excited about?" asked Miriam.

"I'm excited about my first horseback ride," she explained with a shy smile.

"Well," said Sandy, "that does sound like fun, but I'm most interested in the surprise Mr. Virtueson has for us."

In the back of the bus, the boys were just as excited as the girls.

Each mile brought all of them closer to church camp, and soon they would arrive. Then a great week at camp would begin.

. . . and soon a small, sleeping visitor would awake!

"There it is!" yelled Racer.

"I see it too," shouted Happy.

At last, they could all read the signs: MOUNT OLIVE BIBLE CAMP. WELCOME. To the left were the BOYS' CABINS. To the right were the GIRLS' CABINS.

"Yeah! We're here! Now the fun can really start!" squealed Sandy.

"Look at all the other kids. There must be a zillion of them," Happy guessed.

Needless to say, there weren't quite a zillion people there, but there were bus loads and bus loads of excited campers!

Booker was so eager to start the week at camp that he jumped to his feet, along with the other boys, before he remembered: girls first.

"Whoa! We forgot to let the girls go first," he reminded.

"Thank you, Booker," said Miriam as she smiled up at him and made her way to the front of the bus. Booker was very glad he had remembered his manners.

Mr. Friendson and Mr. Virtueson and all the boys helped unload the bags. They even helped carry the girls' suitcases to the door of their cabin before they headed toward the boys' cabin.

The girls had already rushed inside their cabin with Mrs. Virtueson and Miss Content. In lickety-split time, they settled on who would sleep in which bunk.

Then, as girls do, they opened their suitcases, made their beds, and had the cabin looking homey. This was before the boys across the road in the boys' cabin had even decided where each boy would bunk.

It also took longer in the boys' cabin to settle in, for it seemed that EVERY BOY WANTED A TOP BUNK! They didn't unpack their suitcases as the girls did either. Instead, they stuffed them under the beds where their sleeping bags were still rolled up. Without another thought, they headed out the cabin door to get a look around the camp before it got dark.

Since the boys hadn't unpacked their suitcases and bags, they hadn't discovered the little visitor in J. Michael's backpack, but it didn't matter—he was content. He had a supper of nuts and went right back to sleep!

Later that night, as most of the travelers were sleeping soundly in their bunks, Mitchie woke up to the sound of sniffles coming from the bunk below. Susie was crying! Mrs. Virtueson sat in a chair beside

Susie's bunk, trying to comfort her. Mitchie didn't mean to listen, but she did. She really couldn't help hearing.

Susie was crying because she was so unhappy at home. Susie missed her real dad and wasn't sure her mother and stepfather really loved her.

Suddenly, Mitchie didn't feel angry at Susie anymore. Instead, she felt very sorry for her. Mitchie had been wrong to think that Susie was happy just because she had nice clothes and money to spend.

Now Mitchie could see these things did not make Susie or anyone happy. The more important thing was to be loved. It was far better to have a loving family than a basketful of money. It was better to have friends than to have new clothes.

How wrong Mitchie had been. Although Susie had been mean at times, Mitchie had wanted to be like her. All that day, Mitchie had been thinking of Susie's pretty clothes and spending money. Mitchie had been jealous of Susie, instead of being thankful for her own loving family and friends.

Mitchie rolled over, pulling her pillow tighter around her ears. With the pillow shutting out the other voices, Mitchie was in her own silent little world. She asked God to forgive her for being envious. She thanked God for her wonderful family. And then, Mitchie asked God to show Susie how much He loved her. Also, Mitchie asked God to help her be kind to Susie.

As the moon moved across the sky, making way for the coming sun, most of the campers slept peacefully, some even dreaming of the surprise coming tomorrow.

The next morning the mystery visitor in camp woke extra early, had a breakfast of nuts, and began to look for a drink of water . . . .

Summer Surprise

*Rejoice not when thine
enemy falleth.*
Proverbs 24:17

"Look, everybody. Look!" shouted Happy.

"Where? What?" asked Pudge as he sleepily raised his head from his pillow.

"It's moving. J. Michael's backpack is moving!"

All the boys were instantly awake and on their feet, trying to see what Happy had spotted.

"Watch out! Don't touch it!" warned Reginald. "It might be a wild animal or a poisonous snake that got in during the night!"

With that idea, every boy jumped back up on his bunk.

"What is it, Mr. Virtueson?" gasped J. Michael.

"It's the surprise, isn't it?" blurted Booker.

"Yes, that's what it is," they shouted. "It's the surprise, isn't it?"

"Well, fellows," answered Mr. Virtueson. "It's not the surprise. I don't know what's in J. Michael's backpack, but it's not your surprise."

". . . then, what's in there?" asked J. Michael, his eyes big—as were all the eyes watching J. Michael's backpack.

Wondering himself, Mr. Virtueson looked at Mr. Friendson and said, "Please hand me that fishing pole in the corner."

Mr. Friendson handed the fishing pole to Mr. Virtueson, who carefully hooked it through a strap on the backpack and tried to lift the backpack from the floor. The backpack was heavy!

With a thud, it dropped back onto the floor.

Then, whatever was inside the backpack began to move around again.

"Look out! It's moving again!" cried Racer crawling back from the edge of his bunk.

"Calm down, guys. Whatever is in there is small and probably more afraid than all of us put together," said Mr. Friendson.

"Wow, it must really be scared," thought Pudge, whose heart was pounding with excitement.

"Listen," whispered Mr. Friendson. "I can hear it inside the backpack."

All ears tried to catch the smallest sound.

Scratch, scratch.

Chatter, chatter.

Stillness.

Scratch, scratch.

Chatter, chatter.

Now Mr. Virtueson knew what was inside. With a big grin he picked up the backpack and placed it on the edge of the window sill. Slowly, he unzipped the zipper. Everyone was waiting breathlessly to see what was going to come out.

"A squirrel!" squealed Racer as the little creature leaped from the open window to a nearby tree.

Everyone roared with laughter as they remembered how afraid they had just been.

"Hey, Booker, you should have seen yourself," joked Bill.

"Oh, yeah? You looked pretty scared yourself," teased Booker in return.

Meanwhile, the young squirrel chattered and scolded as he jumped to higher and higher limbs. Finally, he looked down from the top of the tree, twitching his tail back and forth.

"How did he get in my backpack?" wondered J. Michael out loud.

"That we'll probably never know," said Ace.

"Perhaps the squirrel got on the bus when we were at the roadside picnic," suggested Reginald.

"More than likely," agreed Mr. Virtueson.

"He probably sniffed out the peanuts in J. Michael's backpack—not expecting to go for a bus ride—and here he is now in a new home," suggested Mr. Friendson.

Then J. Michael had an idea. "Maybe we should pour out the rest of the nuts so that at least he'll have food while he settles into his new home."

As he poured out the peanuts, the little squirrel watched closely, his black eyes shining and his tail twitching. The boys moved away from the window, and the young squirrel inched slowly down the tree, grabbed a peanut, and scurried back to the treetop. He would like his home just fine.

With Mr. Squirrel taken care of, the boys' cabin became a busy place. The campers had lots of things to do and plans to make. They thought they were ready for anything. Would there be any OTHER surprises?

Across the road, the girls' morning had begun much more quietly. Mrs. Virtueson led in prayer and Bible reading. Then giggles and laughter filled the room as the girls began to guess what surprise could be waiting for them!

After breakfast, Mr. Virtueson made an announcement. The "gang" would find out what the surprise was—right after morning services in the big tent.

"Oh," groaned Susie. "I don't like waiting."

"Morning services will be so much fun that you won't even notice having to wait," Christi told her.

Christi's words were true. First, they sang choruses and had a Sword Drill. Then, they listened to a short message about the love of God. When they were dismissed, it was hard to believe that an hour had passed!

Finally, the "gang" gathered around Mr. Virtueson. They begged to know what surprise he had for them.

"Well, we've been asked to present a short play on Friday. The play will be about Baby Moses, how he was found by the Egyptian princess, and how he grew up to be God's leader."

"That sounds like fun!"

"May we get started right away?"

"Whoa!" laughed Mr. Virtueson. "We'll get started right after lunch. Meet me here under the tent, and we'll decide who'll be in the play, who'll make props for the play, who'll sing songs, who'll quote Scripture, and who'll work the spotlights and speakers. For now, let's join the rest of the campers for a hike to the top of the mountain."

As each group of boys and girls began hiking up the mountain path, following one of their leaders, another leader followed behind them, making sure no one got lost or left behind. The boys took a path up the left side of the mountain. The girls took an easier path up the right side of the mountain.

"I don't know what the other path is like," said Sandy, "but this path is really neat. Just look at the many wild flowers!"

"The path the boys took is probably more fun," grumbled Susie. "This path is too easy to climb. It must be for sissies."

Miss Content overheard the girls' conversation. "Just wait until you see the waterfall near the top!" she said.

"I was just thinking how much fun it would be to spend the whole day up here exploring," said Miriam as she stepped over a big rock.

"It doesn't sound like fun to me," said Susie. "I want this hike to be over. I want to get on with the play. I think I should be the princess. With my dark hair and dark eyes, I think I will be perfect."

Susie's words caught Mitchie by surprise. She was thinking she would like to be the Egyptian princess who finds Baby Moses in the Nile River.

"Oh, well, that'll be decided later," she thought. "I don't need to worry right now about who gets chosen."

The rest of the morning went by quickly, and after lunch the "gang" met Mr. Virtueson, just as promised, under the big tent.

They excitedly pulled their chairs into a circle. The play was a wonderful surprise, and everyone was ready to get started! Bill volunteered to work the lights. Reginald would work the speakers and microphones. J. Michael, Booker, and Happy would paint cardboard boxes, making them look like an Egyptian palace and like a river.

Others were hoping to have speaking parts. Not everyone could be a character in the play, of course. Some would need to quote Scripture or sing to make the play more interesting.

But who would be Moses? Who would be Moses' mother? Who would be Pharaoh? Who would be the princess?

"Anyone who wants a speaking part may stay for tryouts," announced Mr. Virtueson. "You will read a few lines from the play; then, Mrs. Virtueson, Miss Content, and Mr. Friendson will decide who should have speaking parts and who should be in the choir. Remember, we are doing this to be a blessing to others and to please the Lord. We must be willing to do what we are asked to do. Not everyone can be Moses or the princess."

Susie leaned over to Mitchie and whispered, "That's right. But I can be the best princess of all."

"Now," continued Mr. Virtueson, "who would like to read the part for Moses or the part for Pharaoh?"

Ace, Racer, and Pudge all raised their hands.

Mr. Virtueson wrote down their names. "Who would like to read for the part of the princess?"

Susie, Sandy, Miriam, and Mitchie raised their hands! Susie frowned at the other girls but said nothing.

"Who would like to be Moses' mother?"

Christi raised her hand.

"Okay!" Mr. Virtueson announced, "Now we'll read for the parts."

The afternoon turned into evening; and, as the boys and girls lined up for supper, they were guessing who would be in the play.

"I think Racer should be Pharaoh," announced Happy.

"Well, Ace would be a good Pharaoh too," added Bill.

"I would like to be Moses," said Pudge, "but my friends also want to have the part. I'm glad I don't have to decide."

"Right," agreed Sandy. "The grownups will be able to decide better than we can."

"Yes," whispered Mitchie to her cousin Miriam, "but I STILL want to be the princess."

Overhearing, Susie spoke up. "I wouldn't count on it, Mitchie. After all, I have a better speaking voice."

Later that evening, Mr. Virtueson announced the parts for the play. Racer would be Moses. Pudge would be Pharaoh. Christi would be Moses' mother . . . and Susie would be the Egyptian princess.

"Mitchie, because you are a good reader, we would like you to be the prompter," announced Mrs. Virtueson. "That means you will sit behind the curtain and read the lines if someone forgets what he or she is supposed to say."

"Ace," continued Mr. Friendson, "you will read Scripture to help tell the story. Everyone else will sing in the choir."

Though not everyone got the part he or she wanted, almost everyone had a good attitude and practiced happily.

There was only one problem as the days passed.

Susie kept bragging that SHE was the princess. She seemed to brag even more when Mitchie was around. "I'm the star," she said over and over.

"I know Jesus wouldn't want me to be angry with Susie," shared Mitchie with Christi one day. "I just don't understand why she acts so mean."

"Susie doesn't know Jesus as Saviour," said Christi. "We must remember to pray for her. We must also remember that, when others do wrong, God still wants us to do right. Mama tells me that when Susie does mean things to me. Sometimes it's hard, but God wants us to do right."

"I'm glad you're my friend, Christi. Ever since the day we started the trip to camp, you've always helped me do right and please God. My grandmother has always told me that a true friend helps you learn more about God's ways. I promise to keep TRYING to be kind to Susie and to forgive her when she acts mean."

"Good for you, Mitchie. Now, let's go over and help Happy paint the cardboard palace. Okay?"

Away the two friends ran, forgetting about what Susie had done.

Paint.

Practice.

Sing.

Practice.

Memorize lines.

Practice.

Soon it was Thursday afternoon. They all knew their lines. Pharaoh Pudge,

Moses Racer, Mother Christi, and Princess Susie had colorful costumes to wear. How grand they looked in front of the cardboard palace beside the cardboard river. How grand they would look on Friday, when all the lights would be out except the big blue spotlight that Bill would shine on them! This play was the best summer surprise they'd ever had.

When they had ended the last practice, Princess Susie and Mother Christi were hanging up their costumes. Sandy, Miriam, and Mitchie were helping.

Susie tilted her head and tossed her hair to one side just to let the other girls know she was so-o-o-o special. She seemed to think she was the perfect princess and that everyone should know princesses are better than other people. Looking at Mitchie she said, "Maybe next time you can be in a play. That is, of course, if you get over being shy so you can speak as well as I do."

"O-o-o-oh," thought Mitchie as she began to shake. "Will I ever be glad when Susie is through being a princess!" She didn't say a word though. She was going to do right.

After services that night, the whole camp was excited about the announcement that something special would happen on the last day. Only the boys and girls from Highland City knew what that special thing would be!

The lights in the cabins were turned out about 10:30. Everywhere, on top bunks and in bottom bunks, campers were thinking about how much fun they were having at church camp. Some were thinking how wonderful it was to have asked the Lord Jesus to forgive them of their sins. Some were thinking how good it was just to know that God loved them.

In the middle of the night, one camper didn't feel well. This one camper had a fever, a headache, and itched all over. Mrs. Virtueson told the camper she would probably feel better in the morning.

Morning came. The girls woke up, and one by one they jumped out of bed.

"Oh! Oh!"

"Look at Susie!"

"Mrs. Virtueson, look at Susie!"

"Susie, look in the mirror!"

Measles! That's what it was. Princess Susie had the measles! Susie would be better in a few days, but this day she would have to stay in bed. And . . . Susie would not be better in time to be the Egyptian princess who found Baby Moses in the Nile River.

Susie cried and said she felt fine, but Susie was not fine, and Mrs. Virtueson put her back to bed. Miss Content agreed to stay with her.

Who would be the princess now? There was only one girl who knew the lines well enough to take Susie's place, and that was Mitchie. She had learned Susie's lines by being the prompter behind the curtain!

When Mrs. Virtueson told Mitchie she would have to be the new princess, Mitchie began to cry.

"Why, Mitchie. I thought you'd be glad to be the Egyptian princess," said Mrs. Virtueson.

Between sobs, Mitchie blurted out, "Ever since I saw all those measles on Susie's face, I was glad. She has been so mean to me. I was glad she got measles and couldn't be the princess. Then I began to be ashamed. Even when you tell me I can be the princess, I'm not happy."

"I understand, Mitchie, but look at this Scripture with me."

Mrs. Virtueson turned to Proverbs 24:17. "'Rejoice not when thine enemy falleth.' That means we are not to be happy when an enemy fails or has trouble."

"You are unhappy," explained Mrs. Virtueson, "because you did something that God has told us not to do. In a way, Susie has been your enemy, and you felt glad when something bad happened to her."

"Yes," agreed Mitchie as she broke into tears again. "I've been so wrong."

"Mitchie, look at another Scripture with me. This Scripture is one that God wrote for everyone who does wrong. I John 1:9. 'If we confess our sins, he [God] is faithful and just to forgive us our sins, and to cleanse us from all unrighteousness.'"

Mitchie knew what she must do. She asked God to forgive her for being glad when Susie got sick and couldn't be the princess. She asked God to forgive her for rejoicing when her enemy fell.

Then Mitchie went into the cabin where Susie was lying on a bottom bunk.

"Susie, I want to ask you to forgive me for feeling bad toward you. I was wrong."

"Aw, it's not your fault I got the measles. I would have been the best princess, but you'll do okay. Next year we can do another play, and I'll be the queen."

Old Clothes, New Clothes, Cowboy Clothes

Pleasant words are . . .
sweet to the soul.
Proverbs 16:24

The sun was very warm, so three little friends sat under the big shade tree in Christi's backyard. Christi, Sandy, and Susie held their favorite dolls as they sat on the old quilt for a pretend picnic.

"Can you believe it is almost time for school to start again?" exclaimed Sandy.

"Yes," replied Christi, "we have had a lot of fun this summer, but I can hardly wait to get back into the Learning Center . . . especially when we get to wear our new uniforms."

"Ugh!" said Susie. "Uniforms! I wouldn't like that! I would much rather go to MY school so I can wear something pretty every day . . . something different."

"Well," replied Christi, "it's fun to dress alike. We have lots of fun when we go on field trips. People can tell we are one happy group. All of the gang looks alike. It's kind of like being a team of friends everywhere we go."

Without saying a word, Susie thought to herself, "I hadn't thought about that."

"Besides," added Sandy, "since my daddy and mother save money because they don't have to buy so many school clothes, they can spend more on special clothes—like church clothes and play clothes."

Without saying a word, and almost wanting to be a student at Highland School, Susie stood up and again thought to herself, "I hadn't thought about that either."

Out loud, Susie asked, "If your daddy and mother save money like that, why does your mother buy some of your clothes at garage sales? I know you have a lot of secondhand dresses, and your little sister Becky wears your hand-me-down clothes all the time."

Then, not waiting for Sandy's answer, Susie spun around and headed out the gate.

"I wanted Susie to stay. I was going to try to put a new verse to work," said Christi.

"Which verse?" asked Sandy.

"Proverbs 16:24: 'Pleasant words are . . . sweet to the soul.' But Susie didn't stay around long enough for me to speak any pleasant words to her. Oh, well, I'll try it when we go over to her house to invite her family to 'Roundup Day' next Sunday."

Christi and Sandy started picking up the toy dishes and their favorite dolls. The afternoon under the big shade tree didn't seem quite so much fun now. It seemed Susie always tried to use hurtful words, even when Christi and Sandy tried to be nice to her.

Knowing her best friend was a little upset, Christi sat back down on the quilt and looked sideways at Sandy. "That verse

is true. Let's both do what it says the next time we see Susie. I know God wants us to be kind and patient with her. Sandy, my daddy and mother think Susie really wants to come to our school. Maybe that's why she was upset when we were talking about dressing alike. I think she really wants to be part of our team of friends."

"I hope Susie will come to Highland School this year," said Sandy. "I feel better already . . . even if she did make fun of our garage-sale clothes."

Christi patted and straightened the quilt. "There's nothing wrong with buying good clothes from someone else. Some people just get tired of a dress and want to get rid of it for no reason. Then, others can buy it for just a little money. Mama says we are being good stewards with God's money if we spend wisely and save as much as we can."

"You mean your mother buys some of your clothes at garage sales too?" asked

Sandy with more than a little bit of surprise on her face.

"Of course!" said Christi with a giggle. "She also fixes my old clothes instead of buying new ones."

Sandy smiled with relief. "My mother does too! I remember once—when I was real little—my favorite dress had a stain on it. I cried when I thought that Mama would have to throw it away. Do you know what she did? She bought a beautiful heart-shaped piece of lace and put it right over the stain! Then, my favorite dress was REALLY my favorite dress."

"Well, I remember a story my mother told me," said Christi, "about when she was a little girl. She had gone to the store with her aunt. Looking around the shelves, she saw a bottle of window cleaner. Mother thought that window cleaner was the prettiest shade of blue she had ever, ever seen.

"Mother didn't know it, but her aunt was watching her. Auntie seemed to know what my mother was thinking. She asked Mother if she would like to have a dress that color of blue.

"'Oh, yes,' squealed my mother. It seems funny to say my mother squealed, but remember, she was just a little girl when this story took place."

"I know. I know," added Sandy, "but hurry! Tell me what happened!"

"Well, later that week, not long before mother's summer visit with her aunt ended, mother heard Auntie running the sewing machine early one morning.

"Mother couldn't help but wonder if Auntie was making her a dress of beautiful blue. Of course, when Auntie came out of the bedroom where she had been sewing, Mother was too polite to ask Auntie WHAT she had been sewing. But Mother was so hopeful."

"Well, what was her Auntie making?" asked Sandy, in a hurry to hear how the story would end. "Was it a dress of the beautiful blue color?"

"Ha!" teased Christi. "Maybe I won't tell you the rest of the story until tomorrow."

"If you don't tell me now," joked Sandy, "my doll may get angry and walk right out that gate."

Then the two friends fell back onto the quilt and laughed and laughed. Sandy wanted to know the end of the story, and Christi thought it was so-o-o-o funny to tease Sandy.

Just then, Mrs. Lovejoy opened the back door and walked toward the two gigglers on the quilt under the big shade tree.

"What is so funny?" she asked with a grin.

"Oh, Mama, I was telling Sandy about the time you went to visit Auntie for the summer and wanted to have a beautiful blue dress the same color as the bottle of blue window cleaner."

"Well, since you and Sandy are laughing so hard, you must not have finished telling the story," added Mrs. Lovejoy.

"What?" said Sandy as she sat straight up on the quilt. "Do you mean your auntie wasn't making a dress of beautiful BLUE just for YOU?"

Then, Mrs. Lovejoy and Christi both had to laugh. Not only was Sandy wanting to hear the end of the story, she was rhyming her words. When the giggles slowed down again, Mother urged Christi to finish the story.

"Oh, Mother, I have laughed so hard, I don't think I can. Would you please finish the story for Sandy? Please hurry so her doll won't get angry and run out the gate!"

Then Christi and Sandy started to laugh again. Mrs. Lovejoy was not sure why the two little gigglers were laughing so hard, but she sat down beside them and waited for them to get over their giggles.

Wiping fun tears from their eyes, Christi and Sandy were soon ready for the end of the story.

"Later that day," continued Mrs. Lovejoy, "I went out to play. Outside, I could hear the sewing machine running again. Oh, how I hoped Auntie was making me a blue dress! After lunch, when I lay down to rest, I heard the sewing machine again! When I woke up from my nap, Auntie called me to come into her room.

"I hurried, and there at the old sewing machine in a room full of old furniture sat Auntie. She held up a little dress of beautiful blue! I ran to her, threw my arms around her, and thanked her over and over.

"Auntie told me to 'run along and try on the dress.' As you can imagine, I didn't have to be told twice. After changing into the new blue dress, I rushed back into my auntie's room. I twirled around in excitement. Round and round I turned, the full skirt of the beautiful blue dress flying out all around me.

"Then, all of a sudden . . . . Rriippppp!"

"Oh, no!" gasped Sandy.

"That's just what I thought," said Mrs. Lovejoy. "The beautiful blue dress had caught on a screw sticking out of the old dresser, right where the knob had fallen off.

"My beautiful blue dress, as new as new could be, was ripped right in front! I burst into tears. Auntie pulled me up onto her lap. In the kindest voice, she began to talk to me. She said she could patch the dress so that the tear would hardly be noticeable.

"Auntie dried my tears and told me that I could learn something very wonderful from my beautiful blue dress. She said the tear on the beautiful blue dress would remind me that people look on the outward appearance but that God looks on our hearts. What we are on the inside is more important. When God looks on the inside, He should see things more beautiful than blue dresses. He should see things like love, joy, and peace.

"Even today, though Auntie has been in Heaven a long time, I remember her words. Clothes aren't as important as I once thought they were." With that said, Mrs. Lovejoy stood up to go back into the house.

"Thank you, Mother, for telling us the story," said Christi. She thought about the new verse she had quoted earlier. *"Pleasant words are . . . sweet to the soul."*

Turning to her friend, Christi said, "Maybe we should go and find out if Susie can come to Roundup Sunday. Maybe my daddy can ask Susie's mother about letting Susie come to Highland School this year."

"That sounds like a good idea," agreed Sandy. "I know Ace's daddy was planning to go see Mr. Vain, Ronny's daddy. Maybe they can see both families! If Susie and Ronny could come to Roundup Sunday and see what a wonderful school we have, maybe they would want to come too!"

Roundup Sunday was a very special Sunday at Highland Church. All the Sunday school classes, all the workers on the bus routes, and all the teachers in Children's Church tried to "round up" all the boys and girls and their families in the neighborhood.

Roundup Sunday was also a time when Pastor Alltruth wanted all the children and all the parents in his town to learn about the school at Highland Church.

The girls knew Pastor Alltruth prayed every day for the families in the little town of Highland City. He loved the people in his town and wanted all the boys and girls to come to a school where they would be loved and where they could learn to live for God.

Later that same night, Mr. Lovejoy and Mr. Virtueson talked on the phone. The two fathers decided that Mr. Lovejoy and Christi should go visit Susie and her mother. Mr. Virtueson and Ace would go visit Ronny's family.

The next morning, Christi called Sandy and Ace called Racer with their news. Both the children and their parents, who had been visited the night before, had agreed to come to Roundup Sunday.

The big day finally came and was beautiful. The weather was turning cooler, and the first leaves were beginning to change from green to red and gold.

Susie had spent the night with Sandy and enjoyed riding the bus to church. Susie's mother had even bought her a new cowgirl costume to wear.

Everyone, it seemed, was dressed like a pioneer or a cowboy or cowgirl. The buses were filled with excited children, and many interested families came in cars. The parking lot beside the church was full!

During the church service, Pastor Alltruth showed a video that told about the best school in the world—Highland School— where the children were loved and God's Word was the best book for learning.

After the morning service, friends and guests gathered outside for a picnic. Many families met Mr. Friendson and the students of Highland School. Some fathers and

mothers enrolled their children that very day.

After the picnic, Susie and her mother said good-bye and started home. As they waved, both Christi and Sandy hoped Susie would come to their church school!

Then, the two friends walked over to join Ace and Racer. Racer was very sad, and Ace was trying to cheer him. Ace looked up at the girls and said, "We're both sad. Ronny just told us he never wants to come to our school. He said he would never want to go to a school where he had to wear a tie."

Racer added, ever so sadly, "Ronny doesn't understand how wearing a shirt with a tie can make you feel special. I feel all grown up when I put on our school uniform."

"But the saddest thing," Ace went on, "is that Ronny won't be in a school where he will learn more about God's love."

Christi and Sandy understood. "We are hoping that Susie will come to Highland

School this year; so, we know just how you feel about Ronny," said Christi.

"Let's pray for them," suggested Sandy.

So right there beside the tables holding leftover hot dogs and glasses of lemonade, two little cowboys and two little cowgirls prayed for their friends.

All in all, Roundup Sunday was a very happy Sunday filled with cowboys and cowgirls of all sizes. Some new families joined the church. And several new students enrolled in the Christian school!

Two weeks later, on a Monday morning warmed with autumn sunshine, the students of Highland School marched into their Learning Centers. All the friends—new and old—looked bright and cheerful in their crisp, new uniforms. The girls smiled with joy, and the boys looked almost as grown up as Mr. Friendson.

After Bible reading, the students pledged to the American flag, the Christian flag, and to the Bible. Then Mr. Friendson led in prayer. Ace and Racer silently prayed for Ronny, while Christi and Sandy silently prayed for Susie.

Each student sat down in his office, excited about the colorful new PACEs filled with wonderful new things to learn. Even Reginald, Bill, Pudge, and Happy were more excited about the new PACEs than they were about break time or lunch! This was going to be the best year ever for Highland School!